LEVEL 1 For first readers

* short, straightforward sentences
* basic, fun vocabulary
* simple, easy-to-follow stories of up to 100 words
* large print and easy-to-read design

LEVEL 2 For developing readers

* longer sentences
* simple vocabulary, introducing new words
* longer stories of up to 200 words
* bold design, to capture readers' interest

LEVEL 3 For more confident readers

* longer sentences with varied structure
* wider vocabulary
* high-interest stories of up to 300 words
* smaller print for experienced readers

LEVEL 4 For able readers

* longer sentences with complex structure
* rich, exciting vocabulary
* complex stories of up to 400 words
* emphasis on text more than illustrations

Make Reading Fun!

Once you have read the story, you will find some amazing activities at the back of the book! There are Excellent Exercises for you to complete, plus a super Picture Dictionary.

But first it is time for the story . . .

Ready?

Steady?

Let's read!

Michael Catchpool   Vanessa Cabban

WHERE THERE'S A BEAR, THERE'S TROUBLE!

LITTLE TIGER PRESS
London

One brown bear saw
one yellow bee.
One yellow bee saw
one brown bear.

One brown bear thought, "Where there's a bee, there must be honey. I'll follow this bee as quietly as can be."

One yellow bee thought, "Where there's a bear, there must be trouble. I'll buzz off home as quietly as can be."

Buzz! Growl! Growl! Shhh!

Two greedy geese spotted one
brown bear. They thought,
"Where there's a bear, there
must be berries."
So two greedy geese
followed one brown bear.
And one brown bear followed
one yellow bee.

Buzz! Growl! Cackle! Shhh!

Three shy mice saw two
greedy geese. "Aha!" they
thought. "Where there are
geese, there must be corn."

So three shy mice followed two greedy geese. Two greedy geese followed one brown bear. One brown bear followed one yellow bee, who flew right into its nest . . .

Buzz! Growl! Cackle! Squeak! Shhh!

. . . and a thousand bees flew out!

"Where there are bees, there
must be trouble!" cried Bear.
"I'll run back home as quickly
as can be."

"Help!" cried the geese. "The bear
is after us!"

"Help!" cried the mice. "The geese are after us!"

Growl! Ouch!

Squawk! Hiss!

Squeak! Eek!

BOUNCE . . .

WOBBLE . . .

One bear fell over two geese.
Two geese fell over three mice.
One yellow bee thought,
"I knew there would be trouble!"

CRASH!

Excellent Exercises

Have you read the story? Well done!
Now it is time for more fun!

Here are some questions about the story. Ask an adult to
listen to your answers, and help if you get stuck.

Bear Hunt

In this story, the bear follows the bee, the geese follow
the bear and the mice follow the geese. Have *you* ever
played a game like that? What was it called?

Buzzy Bees

Can you count all the bees in this picture?

In a Flap

Now describe what is happening in this picture.

Happy Hobby

At the start of the story, the bear decides to follow the bee. Can you remember why?

Picture Dictionary

Can you read all of these words from the story?

bear

bee

brown

fell

geese

mice

one

three

two

yellow

Can you think of any other words that describe these pictures – for example, what colours can you see? Why not try to spell some of these words? Ask an adult to help!

More Fun in Level 2!

Hopping Mad!

Fred has five frogs. Finn has five frogs, too. And when ten frogs get together, it is party time! But Fred and Finn do not find the froggy madness very funny . . .

Newton

Newton keeps hearing funny noises! "Don't be scared!" he tells his toys. And he sets off in the dark to find out what is making the scary sounds.